I Need You, Dear Dragon

by Margaret Hillert

Illustrated by Jack Pullan

NORWOOD HOUSE PRESS

DEAR CAREGIVER,

The books in this Beginning-to-Read collection may look somewhat familiar in that the original versions could have been a part of your own early reading experiences. These carefully written texts feature common sight words to provide your child multiple exposures to the words appearing most frequently in written text. These new versions have been updated and the engaging illustrations are highly appealing to a contemporary audience of young readers.

Begin by reading the story to your child, followed by letting him or her read familiar words and soon your child will be able to read the story independently. At each step of the way, be sure to praise your reader's efforts to build his or her confidence as an independent reader. Discuss the pictures and encourage your child to make connections between the story and his or her own life. At the end of the story, you will find reading activities and a word list that will help your child practice and strengthen beginning reading skills. These activities, along with the comprehension questions are aligned to current standards, so reading efforts at home will directly support the instructional goals in the classroom.

Above all, the most important part of the reading experience is to have fun and enjoy it!

Shannon Cannon

Shannon Cannon,
Literacy Consultant

Norwood House Press • www.norwoodhousepress.com
Beginning-to-Read™ is a registered trademark of Norwood House Press.
Illustration and cover design copyright ©2017 by Norwood House Press. All Rights Reserved.

Authorized adapted reprint from the U.S. English language edition, entitled I Need You, Dear Dragon by Margaret Hillert. Copyright © 2017 Margaret Hillert. Reprinted with permission. All rights reserved. Pearson and I Need You, Dear Dragon are trademarks, in the US and/or other countries, of Pearson Education, Inc. or its affiliates. This publication is protected by copyright, and prior permission to re-use in any way in any format is required by both Norwood House Press and Pearson Education. This book is authorized in the United States for use in schools and public libraries.

LIBRARY OF CONGRESS CATALOGING-IN-PUBLICATION DATA

Names: Hillert, Margaret, author. I Pullan, Jack, illustator.
Title: I need you, Dear Dragon / by Margaret Hillert ; illustrated by Jack Pullan.
Description: Chicago, IL : Norwood House Press, 2016. I Series: A
  Beginning-to-read book I Summary: "Dear Dragon feels rejected when a new
  baby arrives. Love and reassurance put him at ease as he finds new ways to
  help with the new addition to the family. Completely re-illustrated from
  original edition. Includes reading activities and a word list"-- Provided
  by publisher.
Identifiers: LCCN 2015046735 (print) I LCCN 2016009467 (ebook) I ISBN
  9781599537719 (library edition : alk. paper) I ISBN 9781603578974 (eBook)
Subjects: I CYAC: Babies--Fiction. I Dragons--Fiction.
Classification: LCC PZ7.H558 Iam 2016 (print) I LCC PZ7.H558 (ebook) I DDC
  [E]--dc23
LC record available at http://lccn.loc.gov/2015046735

288N—072016
Manufactured in the United States of America in North Mankato, Minnesota.

Here comes the car.
Oh, here comes the car.
I see Mother.
Mother is home.

Mother, Mother.
Now you are home.
This is good.

Is that the baby?
I want to see her.
Oh, I want to see her!

Oh, my.
Oh, my.
A little, little baby.

What a pretty baby!
What a pretty baby she is.
Look, look!

In here.
In here.
This is where we go.

This is something for
the baby—

and this—

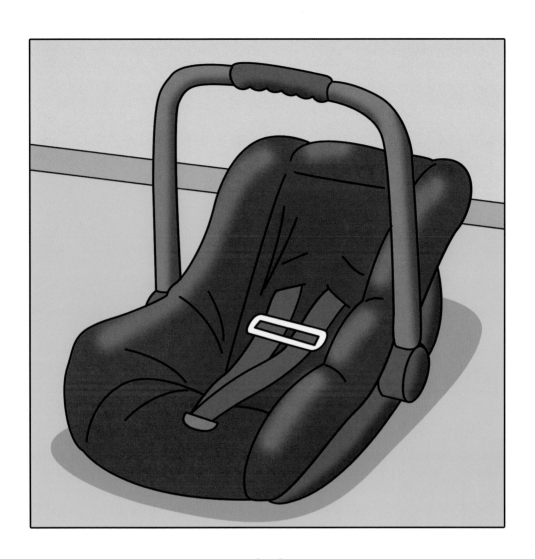

and this.

Father, Father.
Can I have the baby?
I want the baby.

My, what a pretty one.
So little, so little.
I like you, little baby.

Here, Mother.
This is a good little baby.
I like her.

Oh, there you are.
You did not come in.
We want you to come in.

See.
Here is something
that looks like you.
It is for the baby.

BABY
POWDER

The baby will like it.
Yes, yes.
The baby will like it.

Come here.
Come here.
You can do something here.
Come on.
Come on.

See now.
Look what you can do.
This is a good thing for
you to do.

Look at that.
The baby likes you.
And I like you, too.
I do.
I do!

The baby is little.
Too little to play with me now.
But you and I can play.

We can play and have fun.
Come on with me.
Come on and play.
Run, run, run!

Here you are with me.
And here I am with you.
I need you.
I need you, Dear Dragon.

The following activities support the findings of the National Reading Panel that determined the most effective components for reading instruction are: Phonemic Awareness, Phonics, Vocabulary, Fluency, and Text Comprehension.

Phonemic Awareness: The /y/ sound

Oral Blending: Say the beginning and ending sounds of the following words and ask your child to listen to the sounds and say the whole word:

/y/ + ou = you	/y/ + es = yes	/y/ + ear = year
/y/ + am = yam	/y/ + arn = yarn	/y/ + uck = yuck
/y/ + ard = yard	/y/ + ellow = yellow	

Phonics: The letter Yy

1. Demonstrate how to form the letters **Y** and **y** for your child.
2. Have your child practice writing **Y** and **y** at least three times each.
3. Ask your child to point to the words in the book that have the letter **y** in them.
4. Write down the following words and ask your child to circle the letter **y** in each word:

yes	you	baby	my	funny
money	key	young	cycle	pretty
your	silly	cry	maybe	yard

Vocabulary: Adjectives

1. Explain to your child that words that describe something are called adjectives.
2. Say the following nouns and ask your child to name an adjective that might be used to describe it (possible answers in parentheses):

car (fast)	flower (pretty)	candy (sweet)
snake (slimy)	clown (funny)	sun (bright)
cotton (soft)	mansion (big)	ice (cold)

3. Ask your child to name the adjectives that might be used to describe babies. (Possible answers: pretty, tiny, cute, cuddly, sweet, soft, wiggly, little, chubby, noisy, etc.)

4. Write the words on separate pieces of paper.

5. Mix the words up and read each word aloud to your child. Encourage your child to explain how the adjective describes babies.

6. Mix the words up again and randomly say each word to your child. Ask your child to point to the correct word.

Fluency: Shared Reading

1. Reread the story to your child at least two more times while your child tracks the print by running a finger under the words as they are read. Ask your child to read the words he or she knows with you.

2. Reread the story taking turns, alternating readers between sentences or pages.

Text Comprehension: Discussion Time

1. Ask your child to retell the sequence of events in the story.

2. To check comprehension, ask your child the following questions:
   • Where do you think the boy's mother and father were?
   • What are the things the family has for the baby on pages 11–13?
   • How does the boy feel about having a new baby in the family? How do you know?
   • How does Dear Dragon help the baby?
   • Do you think you would make a good big brother or sister? Why?

WORD LIST

I Need You, Dear Dragon uses the 61 words listed below.

This list can be used to practice reading the words that appear in the text. You may wish to write the words on index cards and use them to help your child build automatic word recognition. Regular practice with these words will enhance your child's fluency in reading connected text.

a	Father	like(s)	run	want
am	for	little		we
and	fun	look(s)	see	what
are			she	where
at	go	me	so	will
	good	Mother	something	with
baby		my		
but	have		that	yes
	her	need	the	you
can	here	not	there	
car	home	now	thing	
come(s)			this	
	I	oh	to	
dear	in	on	too	
did	is	one		
do	it			
dragon		play		
		pretty		

ABOUT THE AUTHOR Margaret Hillert has helped millions of children all over the world learn to read independently. She was a first grade teacher for 34 years and during that time started writing books that her students could both gain confidence in reading and enjoy. She wrote well over 100 books for children just learning to read. As a child, she enjoyed writing poetry and continued her poetic writings as an adult for both children and adults.

Photograph by Glenna Washburn

ABOUT THE ILLUSTRATOR A talented and creative illustrator, Jack Pullan, is a graduate of William Jewell College. He has also studied informally at Oxford University and the Kansas City Art Institute. He was mentored by the renowned watercolor artists, Jim Hamil and Bill Amend. Jack's work has graced the pages of many enjoyable children's books, various educational materials, cartoon strips, as well as many greeting cards. Jack currently resides in Kansas.